Enchanted Shadows-A Forbidden Desire

SMAE

Published by SMAE, 2024.

ENCHANTED SHADOWS-A FORBIDDEN DESIRE

First edition. June 20, 2024.

ISBN: 979-8227436924

Written by SMAE.

To those who dare to explore the shadows within and find the light that guides them through.

To my family and friends, for your unwavering support and belief in my dreams.

And to every reader who embarks on this journey with Eva, may you find the strength to embrace your own magic and face the darkness with courage and hope.

Chapter 1: The Spellbook

Eva Blackwood's fingers brushed the ancient, dust-covered spine of the forbidden spellbook. Hidden away in the deepest recesses of the magical academy's library, the book seemed to pulse with a life of its own, calling to her. She had always felt out of place in the magical world, her abilities stronger and darker than those of her peers. The allure of the unknown, the thrill of the forbidden, tugged at her soul as she carefully pulled the book from the shelf.

The room was dimly lit, casting long shadows that danced around her as she flipped through the brittle, yellowed pages. Symbols and incantations of a dark nature filled the book, promising power, and knowledge beyond her wildest dreams. As she read, a strange sense of connection washed over her, as if the book were an extension of her desires.

Her heart raced with excitement and trepidation. What if someone caught her? The consequences would be severe, but the temptation was too great to resist. She could feel the magic in her veins, responding to the words on the pages, awakening something deep and primal within her.

A soft, velvety voice interrupted her thoughts. "You shouldn't be here, Eva."

Eva whirled around to find Lysander Thorn standing in the doorway, his dark eyes piercing through the shadows. Tall and brooding, with an air of mystery surrounding him, Lysander was known for his expertise in forbidden magic. He had always kept his distance from the other students, his past shrouded in secrecy. Now, he seemed more enigmatic than ever as he stepped closer.

"I couldn't help myself," Eva admitted, her voice barely above a whisper. "This book... it's like it's calling to me."

Lysander's gaze softened, though a flicker of concern remained. "The power it holds is dangerous, Eva. It can consume you if you are not careful."

Eva looked down at the spellbook, her fingers tracing the intricate symbols. "But what if it is what I need to finally belong? To understand who I am?"

Lysander sighed, running a hand through his dark hair. "I know the allure. I have been where you are now. But you must tread carefully. Let me help you."

Eva's heart skipped a beat at his offer. She had always admired Lysander from afar, drawn to his strength and the mystery that surrounded him. Now, with his dark eyes fixed on hers, she felt an undeniable connection, a spark that ignited something deep within her.

"All right," she agreed, closing the spellbook with a decisive thud. "Teach me."

Eva sat in a secluded alcove of the library; her eyes fixed on the spellbook's pages while Lysander's deep voice guided her through the intricacies of a particularly complex incantation. His presence was magnetic, and every word he spoke seemed to resonate with an unspoken promise of power and understanding. She found herself drawn not only to the dark magic but also to the enigmatic man who wielded it with such confidence.

"Concentrate, Eva," Lysander said softly, his breath warm against her ear. "You must control the power, not let it control you."

Eva nodded, closing her eyes to focus. She could feel the energy swirling around her, a dark, seductive force that promised to fulfill her deepest desires. As she whispered the incantation, the air crackled with magic, and she felt a surge of power rush through her veins. When she opened her eyes, a shimmering barrier of dark energy surrounded her, a perfect execution of the spell Lysander had taught her.

"Impressive," Lysander murmured, his voice laced with admiration. "You have a natural talent for this."

Eva's heart raced, both from the exhilaration of casting the spell and the intense gaze Lysander fixed upon her. She had never felt more powerful, more alive. But as the barrier faded, she noticed a figure watching from the shadows.

"Who's there?" she called out, her voice steady despite the sudden jolt of fear.

A student stepped forward, eyes wide with a mix of awe and apprehension. "What are you doing, Eva? That spell... it's forbidden."

Eva's mind raced. She knew the students would report what they had seen. Before she could respond, Lysander stepped in front of her, his expression darkening.

"Leave us," he commanded, his voice brooking no argument. The student hesitated for a moment before scurrying away, leaving Eva and Lysander alone once more.

"You need to be more careful," Lysander said, turning back to her. "There are those who would not understand."

Eva nodded, the reality of their situation sinking in. She was treading a dangerous path, but the thrill of it, the connection she felt with Lysander, made it impossible to turn back now.

In the days that followed, Eva's mastery of dark magic grew under Lysander's tutelage. The spells she learned were more powerful and more dangerous than anything she had ever encountered. Each success brought a rush of exhilaration, a feeling of invincibility that only deepened her desire to explore the spellbook further.

During a particularly intense lesson, Lysander introduced her to a spell that manipulated shadows. "This is not just about control," he explained. "It's about becoming one with the darkness."

Eva's pulse quickened as she repeated the incantation. The shadows around her seemed to come alive, swirling and twisting at her command. She could feel their power coursing through her, an intoxicating mix of fear and desire. As the spell reached its climax, the shadows solidified into a dark, menacing form that hovered before her, obedient to her will.

Lysander watched with a mixture of pride and caution. "You have an extraordinary gift, Eva. But remember, this power comes with great responsibility. It can consume you if you're not careful."

Eva nodded; her eyes still fixed on the shadowy figure she had conjured. She knew he was right, but the allure of the dark magic was too strong to resist. As the shadows dissipated, she felt a strange sense of satisfaction, a hunger for more.

That evening, as she walked back to her dormitory, she felt the weight of several eyes on her. Whispers followed her, and she knew that her growing prowess in dark magic had not gone unnoticed. She tried to brush off the unease, but a nagging feeling persisted. She was playing with fire, and the boundaries between right and wrong were becoming increasingly blurred.

Eva's newfound abilities began to strain her relationship with Seraphina. One afternoon, as they sat in the potion lab, Seraphina could not hold back her concerns any longer.

"Eva, what are you doing with Lysander?" she asked, her voice filled with worry. "Everyone's talking about the spells you've been casting. They're dangerous."

Eva sighed, frustration bubbling to the surface. "Sera, you don't understand. This magic... it makes me feel alive like I finally belong somewhere."

"But at what cost?" Seraphina pressed. "I'm worried about you. This isn't like you."

Eva met her friend's gaze, seeing the genuine concern in her eyes. She wanted to explain the thrill, the power, the connection she felt with Lysander, but words failed her. Instead, she shook her head. "I can handle it. Lysander is teaching me how to control it."

Seraphina frowned, her worry deepening. "I just hope you know what you're doing. I don't want to see you get hurt."

The conversation left Eva feeling torn. She valued Seraphina's friendship, but the pull of dark magic and her growing bond with Lysander were too powerful to ignore. As she returned to her dormitory, she resolved to be more cautious, but her determination to master the forbidden spells remained unshaken.

Professor Alaric Voss stood at the front of the classroom, his stern gaze sweeping over the students. His presence commanded respect, and the air in the room seemed to crackle with tension. As Eva settled into her seat, she could not shake the feeling that he knew more about her activities than he let on.

"Miss Blackwood," Voss called, his voice cutting through the silence. "A word after class."

Eva's heart skipped a beat, but she nodded, trying to maintain her composure. When the class ended, she approached Voss's desk, her palms sweaty with anxiety.

"You've been spending a lot of time with Mr. Thorn," Voss said, not looking up from his papers. "And dabbling in some very dangerous magic, I hear."

Eva swallowed hard. "I'm just trying to learn, Professor."

Voss finally looked up, his eyes piercing and unreadable. "Knowledge is a double-edged sword, Miss Blackwood. Be careful it doesn't cut you."

His words lingered in her mind long after she left the classroom. There was something in his tone, a hidden meaning that she could not quite decipher. The encounter left her feeling uneasy, but it also fueled her determination to prove herself.

That evening, Eva found herself drawn to the secluded tower where Lysander often retreated. She climbed the winding stairs, her heart pounding with anticipation. When she reached the top, she found Lysander staring out over the dark forest, his expression contemplative.

"You came," he said softly, turning to face her.

Eva nodded, stepping closer. The air between them crackled with tension, the unspoken words hanging heavy. "I can't stop thinking about magic. About us."

Lysander's eyes darkened, and he took a step closer, his hand brushing against hers. "Eva, this path is dangerous. But I can't deny the connection between us."

Their lips met in a heated kiss, the intensity of their emotions bursting forth. It was a moment of pure passion, a merging of their desires and fears. As they pulled away, breathless, Eva knew that there was no turning back. Their fates were intertwined, bound by the dark magic that connected them.

The spellbook lay open on Eva's desk, its pages filled with dark secrets and ancient incantations. As she studied it, she could not help but feel a deepening fascination with its origins. The book had a life of its own, its power calling to her with an irresistible allure.

Lysander had told her that the book was older than the academy itself, a relic from a time when dark magic was not just forbidden, but revered. It was said to have been created by an ancient sorcerer whose name had been lost to history, a master of shadows and desire.

As Eva delved deeper into the book, she uncovered more about its creator and the dark history associated with it. The sorcerer had been a figure of great power, but also great tragedy, his life a testament to the seductive danger of forbidden magic. The more she read, the more she felt a connection to him, as if his spirit were guiding her.

The revelations only fueled her desire to learn more, to master the spells that had once been his. She could feel the magic growing within her, a dark, seductive force that promised power and fulfillment. But with each new spell, the risks grew greater, and the line between right and wrong blurred more.

Seraphina paced the length of their shared dormitory, her worry for Eva intensifying. She had noticed the changes in her friend, the way her eyes seemed to darken with each passing day, the strange aura that surrounded her.

"Eva, we need to talk," Seraphina said, her voice tinged with desperation.

Eva looked up from the spellbook, her expression unreadable. "What is it, Sera?"

"I found something," Seraphina said, pulling a dusty tome from her bag. "About Professor Voss. He has a personal interest in the forbidden spells. There's a connection between him and the spellbook."

Eva frowned; her curiosity piqued. "What do you mean?"

Seraphina opened the tome, revealing pages filled with old, faded notes. "Voss has been studying forbidden magic for years. He is not just interested in controlling it; he wants to harness its power for himself. You need to be careful, Eva. He's dangerous."

Eva's mind raced. The pieces of the puzzle were starting to come together, but there were still so many unanswered questions. She knew she had to be cautious, but the lure of the dark magic and her growing bond with Lysander made it difficult to turn back.

As Eva continued her lessons with Lysander, another figure began to take an interest in her. Cassian Draven, with his charm and dark allure, was a force to be reckoned with. He watched her with a predatory gaze, his intentions unclear but undeniably dangerous.

One evening, as Eva practiced a particularly difficult spell, Cassian approached her. "Impressive," he said, his voice smooth and inviting. "You have quite the talent for dark magic."

Eva looked up, meeting his intense gaze. "What do you want, Cassian?"

He smiled, a hint of danger in his eyes. "Just to get to know you better. Lysander isn't the only one who can teach you about forbidden magic."

Eva felt a shiver run down her spine. There was something about Cassian that set her on edge but also intrigued her. She knew he was a rival to Lysander, but the promise of more knowledge and power was tempting.

"Be careful, Eva," Lysander had warned her. "Cassian is not to be trusted."

But the more time she spent with Lysander, the more she felt torn between the two men. Each offered something different, something dangerous and exciting. And as Cassian's interest in her grew, so did the tension between him and Lysander.

The moon hung high in the sky as Eva stood at the edge of the dark forest, the spellbook clutched in her hands. This was the moment of truth, the pivotal point where she had to decide whether to continue down the dark path she had chosen or heed the warnings of those around her.

Lysander stood beside her, his expression a mix of concern and determination. "Eva, you don't have to do this. There's still time to turn back."

Eva looked at him, her heart torn. "I know, but I can't stop now. The power, the magic... it's a part of me."

Lysander took her hand, his grip firm. "Whatever happens, I'll be here for you."

As Eva began the incantation, the air around her seemed to pulse with energy. The shadows lengthened, and the forest came alive with dark magic. She could feel the power surging through her, a heady mix of fear and exhilaration.

But as the spell reached its climax, a figure emerged from the darkness. Professor Voss, his eyes glowing with a sinister light, stepped forward. "Eva, stop this madness."

The confrontation was inevitable, the clash of wills and magic a testament to the choices Eva had made. The chapter ended with a cliffhanger, leaving the fate of Eva, Lysander, and the forbidden magic hanging in the balance.

Chapter 2: Forbidden Lessons

Eva's days became a blur of intense study and secret meetings with Lysander. The allure of dark magic was intoxicating, and the time she spent with him only deepened her connection to both the power and the man teaching her to wield it.

One evening, as the sun dipped below the horizon, casting long shadows across the academy, Eva met Lysander in their usual spot—a secluded alcove hidden from prying eyes. The air was thick with the promise of another forbidden lesson, and Eva's heart raced with anticipation.

"Today, we delve deeper," Lysander said, his voice a low, seductive whisper. "The spells we will explore are not for the faint of heart. They require absolute focus and control."

Eva nodded; her eyes locked on his. "I'm ready."

Lysander's gaze softened, a flicker of concern in his dark eyes. "Before we begin, you should know more about me. About why I tread this dangerous path."

Eva listened intently as Lysander began to recount his story. He spoke of his early days at the academy, his initial fascination with magic, and the moment he discovered the forbidden spellbook that changed his life forever. He described the power he felt, the allure of the dark spells, and the consequences that followed.

"I lost myself in the magic," Lysander admitted, his voice tinged with regret. "It consumed me, drove me to do things I never thought possible. But I found a way back. A way to control it."

Eva's heart ached at his words. She could see the pain in his eyes, the struggle he endured. "And now you're helping me," she said softly.

Lysander nodded. "I don't want you to make the same mistakes I did. But the power you seek is dangerous. It can give you everything you desire, but it can also take everything away."

Eva reached out, her fingers brushing against his. "I trust you, Lysander. I know the risks, and I'm willing to take them."

Their hands lingered together, a silent promise of support and understanding. As the lesson began, the bond between them grew stronger, their fates intertwined by the dark magic they both craved.

As their lessons progressed, Lysander introduced Eva to increasingly powerful and dangerous spells. One evening, under the pale light of the crescent moon, he taught her a spell that could manipulate the very essence of life itself. The incantation was complex, and the power it promised was immense.

"Focus on your intent," Lysander instructed, his voice steady. "This spell requires absolute precision. One mistake and the consequences could be dire."

Eva closed her eyes, drawing on the deep well of magic within her. She could feel the power building, a heady mix of exhilaration and fear. As she whispered the incantation, she felt the energy surge through her, bending to her will. When she opened her eyes, a small, glowing orb of light hovered between her hands, pulsing with life.

"Perfect," Lysander breathed, his eyes filled with pride and something deeper. "You are truly gifted, Eva."

The rush of power was intoxicating, and Eva felt an undeniable bond with Lysander. But as the orb faded, she could not shake the feeling of being watched.

Later that night, Seraphina confronted her again. "Eva, this has to stop. The magic you're using—it's too dangerous. You're changing, and I'm scared for you."

Eva sighed, torn between her best friend's concern and her thirst for power. "I know you're worried, Sera. But this is something I need to do. Lysander is helping me control it."

Seraphina's eyes were filled with worry. "Just promise me you'll be careful."

Eva nodded, but she knew the path she was on was anything but safe.

That night, Lysander was haunted by dreams of his past. He saw himself as a young wizard, eager and ambitious, discovering the forbidden spellbook for the first time. The power had consumed him, driving him to the brink of madness. He relived the moments of his greatest triumphs and deepest regrets, the lines between them blurring until he could no longer distinguish right from wrong.

He woke with a start, the weight of his past pressing heavily on his chest. Eva, sensing his turmoil, reached out to him. "Lysander, what's wrong?"

He shook his head, trying to dispel the memories. "Just a bad dream. My past... it still haunts me."

Eva took his hand, her touch grounding him. "You're not alone anymore. We'll face this together."

Their bond grew stronger in that moment, transcending the boundaries of mentor and student. They were partners, allies in the dark world of forbidden magic, and their connection was undeniable.

As days turned into weeks, Cassian Draven's interest in Eva became more overt. He watched her with a predatory gaze, his intentions clear. One afternoon, as Eva practiced a difficult spell, Cassian approached her.

"You're quite talented," he said, his voice smooth and seductive. "But there's so much more you could learn. Lysander isn't the only one who can teach you."

Eva felt a shiver run down her spine. Cassian's charm was undeniable, but there was a darkness in his eyes that unsettled her. "What are you getting at, Cassian?"

He smiled, a dangerous glint in his eyes. "Just think about it. There's power in choices, and you have more than one path before you."

The tension between Cassian and Lysander grew palpable, each man representing different aspects of the dark magic that fascinated Eva. She found herself torn, drawn to the power and allure of both men, each offering something the other could not.

Professor Voss's suspicions about Eva and Lysander deepened. He watched them closely, his keen eyes missing nothing. One evening, he called Eva to his office.

"Miss Blackwood," he began, his tone deceptively calm. "I understand you've been spending a lot of time with Mr. Thorn. I hope you realize the dangers of the path you're on."

Eva met his gaze, refusing to show fear. "I'm aware of the risks, Professor. But I trust Lysander. He's helping me."

Voss leaned back, his expression unreadable. "Be careful, Eva. Power can be a seductive force, but it often comes at a great cost."

The warning lingered in her mind as she left his office. Despite the growing danger, Eva couldn't deny her attraction to Lysander. Their connection was intense, their shared passion for forbidden magic drawing them closer together.

Seraphina, determined to protect her friend, delved deeper into the mysteries of the spellbook. She uncovered a dangerous secret: the book was not just a collection of spells, but a living entity, feeding on the desires of those who used it. The more one delved into its pages, the more it ensnared them, binding their fate to its dark power.

She rushed to find Eva, desperate to share her discovery. "Eva, you need to hear this. The spellbook—it's alive. It's feeding on your magic, your desires. It's not just dangerous; it's a trap."

Eva listened, her heart pounding. The revelation was shocking, but it only intensified her resolve. "I can't stop now, Sera. I'm too far in. But I'll be careful, I promise."

That night, as the moonlight streamed through the window, Eva and Lysander shared a moment of intense passion. Their connection, both magical and physical, solidified as they embraced the darkness together. The boundaries between them blurred, their fates entwined in the shadows of forbidden magic.

Chapter 3: Shadows of the Past

Eva sat across from Lysander in the dimly lit alcove, the spellbook open between them. The flickering candlelight cast shadows on his face, highlighting the depth of his inner turmoil. As he spoke, Eva listened intently, eager to understand the man who had become her mentor and more.

"I wasn't always this way," Lysander began, his voice heavy with regret. "There was a time when I was just like you—curious, ambitious, eager to learn. But the spellbook changed everything. It promised power, and I was too blinded by ambition to see the danger."

He paused, his eyes distant as he relived the memories. "The magic consumed me, drove me to the brink of madness. I did things I'm not proud of, things that haunt me to this day. It took everything I had to pull myself back, to regain control."

Eva reached out, her hand gently resting on his. "You're not alone, Lysander. We'll face this together."

Lysander's gaze softened, his eyes filled with gratitude. "I just want you to be careful, Eva. The power you seek comes at a great cost."

As they delved deeper into the spellbook, Eva felt a strange mix of fear and excitement. The spells they uncovered were more powerful than anything she had ever imagined, each one a step further into the darkness.

Seraphina watched from a distance, her heart heavy with worry. She had tried to warn Eva, but her friend seemed too far gone, too enamored with the power and the man guiding her. Seraphina knew she had to protect herself, even if it meant distancing herself from Eva.

One evening, as Eva and Lysander studied a particularly dangerous spell, Cassian approached. His presence was like a dark cloud, and Eva felt a shiver run down her spine.

"Impressive work," Cassian said, his voice smooth and enticing. "But did Lysander tell you everything? Did he mention the true cost of these spells?"

Eva glanced at Lysander, uncertainty flickering in her eyes. "What are you talking about, Cassian?"

Cassian smiled, a dangerous glint in his eyes. "There are secrets Lysander hasn't told you, power he hasn't shared. If you want to learn more, you should come to me."

Eva's mind raced. Could she trust Cassian? He represented everything Lysander warned her about, yet his words held a tempting promise of power and knowledge.

Professor Voss intensified his investigation, his suspicions about Eva and Lysander growing stronger. He watched them closely, his sharp mind piecing together the clues.

One night, as Eva and Lysander practiced a particularly powerful spell, Voss's presence became known. "Miss Blackwood, Mr. Thorn," he called out, his voice cold and authoritative. "What exactly do you think you're doing?"

Eva's heart pounded, but she stood her ground. "We're just studying, Professor."

Voss's eyes narrowed. "Studying forbidden magic is a dangerous path, Eva. One that could lead to disastrous consequences."

As Voss's warnings echoed in her mind, Eva couldn't help but question Lysander's true motives. Was he really helping her, or was he leading her down a path of no return?

Meanwhile, Seraphina uncovered a dark secret about her own family. As she delved into her family's history, she discovered a connection to the spellbook and the dark magic it contained. Her ancestors had been involved in its creation, binding their fate to its power.

Desperate to protect Eva, Seraphina sought her out. "Eva, I found something. My family... we're connected to the spellbook. It's part of our legacy, and it's dangerous."

Eva listened, her mind reeling with the revelation. "What does this mean, Sera?"

"It means we're both entangled in this, more than we ever realized," Seraphina said, her voice trembling. "We have to be careful."

As Eva grappled with this new information, her relationship with Lysander faced new challenges. The trust they had built was tested as the dangers around them grew.

The tension between Lysander and Cassian reached a boiling point. One evening, as they argued over the best way to protect Eva, their disagreement escalated into a confrontation.

"You can't trust him, Eva," Lysander insisted, his voice filled with anger. "Cassian only wants to use you for his own gain."

"And what about you?" Cassian retorted, his eyes blazing. "Are you any different? You've been hiding things from her, keeping her in the dark."

Eva stood between them, torn and confused. "Stop it, both of you. I need to know the truth. No more secrets."

As the lines between ally and enemy blurred, Eva faced a difficult choice. Whom could she trust in this world of shadows and dark magic? The stakes were higher than ever, and every decision could mean the difference between salvation and destruction.

Chapter 4: The Darkening

The atmosphere at the magical academy grew tense as whispers of a dark magic threat spread among the students and faculty. The once vibrant hallways now seemed shrouded in an ominous aura, and a sense of unease permeated the air. Eva and Lysander, aware of the growing danger, tried to stay under the radar while continuing their exploration of the spellbook.

During a quiet evening in their secluded alcove, Eva and Lysander pored over the ancient tome, their heads bent close together. "We need to be careful," Lysander whispered, his eyes scanning the pages. "The academy is on high alert. We can't afford to draw any more attention to ourselves."

Eva nodded, her heart pounding with a mix of fear and excitement. "I know. But we can't stop now. We're so close to uncovering the truth."

As they continued their studies, they discovered spells that were even more powerful and dangerous than those they had learned before. Each incantation pulled them deeper into the web of dark magic, and the boundaries between right and wrong became increasingly blurred.

Eva's powers grew stronger, but with that strength came unpredictability. During a routine class, she accidentally unleashed a burst of dark energy that sent a wave of fear through her fellow students. Whispers followed her wherever she went, and the fear in their eyes was palpable.

Cassian seized the opportunity to further his own agenda. He approached Eva with a charming smile, his intentions clear. "You know, Eva, Lysander isn't the only one who can help you. I can teach you to control your powers, to harness them fully."

Eva hesitated, torn between her loyalty to Lysander and the seductive promise of power that Cassian offered. "What do you want from me, Cassian?"

He leaned in closer, his voice a low murmur. "I want to help you reach your full potential. Together, we could be unstoppable."

Despite her reservations, Eva felt a pull towards Cassian's offer. The power he promised was tempting, and the chaos around her made it difficult to think clearly.

Seraphina's own struggle with dark magic intensified as she tried to help Eva. The more she delved into the mysteries of the spellbook, the more she felt its corrupting influence. Her nights were plagued with nightmares, and her days were filled with an overwhelming sense of dread.

One afternoon, Seraphina confronted Professor Voss, her suspicions about his involvement in the dark magic conspiracy growing. "Professor, I've seen the way you look at Eva and Lysander. What are you hiding?"

Voss's expression remained inscrutable, but there was a flicker of something dark in his eyes. "Miss Nightshade, you should be careful where you tread. There are forces at play here that you do not understand."

Seraphina's heart pounded as she realized the depth of the conspiracy. Voss was more deeply involved than she had initially thought, and his intentions were far from benign.

Lysander and Eva continued their quest for knowledge, and their efforts led them to a hidden chamber deep within the academy. The chamber was filled with ancient artifacts and scrolls, each one holding secrets about the spellbook and its creator.

As they explored the chamber, they discovered a powerful vision spell. "This spell will show us the truth," Lysander said, his voice filled with anticipation. "Are you ready?"

Eva nodded, her heart racing. "Let's do it."

They cast the spell together, and the world around them shifted. They were transported to a time long past, where they witnessed the creation of the spellbook and the dark forces that had shaped its power. The vision was overwhelming, revealing the true nature of the magic they had been dabbling in and the dangers that lay ahead.

The academy was thrown into turmoil as the dark magic threat grew more pronounced. Students and faculty alike were on edge, and the once orderly environment descended into chaos. Eva and Lysander knew that they had to act quickly to confront the forces that sought to control them.

"We need to prepare for the final confrontation," Lysander said, his voice determined. "The dark forces won't stop until they've consumed everything."

Eva nodded, her resolve steeling. "We'll face them together. We can't let the darkness win."

As they gathered their strength and prepared for the battle ahead, they knew that the fate of the academy—and their own futures—hung in the balance. The darkening shadows threatened to consume them, but they were determined to fight back and reclaim their destiny.

Chapter 5: Unraveling Secrets

Eva's choice during the battle had far-reaching consequences, impacting everyone around her. The academy was in disarray, with students and faculty dealing with the aftermath of the conflict. Relationships were strained, and trust was hard to come by. Eva felt the weight of her decision bearing down on her, knowing that her actions had set events in motion that could not be easily undone.

Her friends looked at her differently, some with admiration for her bravery, others with suspicion and fear. Seraphina, in particular, seemed distant, her struggles with dark magic creating a rift between them. The atmosphere at the academy was tense, and Eva knew that the path ahead would be fraught with challenges.

Determined to understand the full scope of the spellbook's power and origins, Eva delved deeper into its pages. The more she read, the more she realized that the book was not merely a collection of spells, but a key to a much larger mystery. It spoke of ancient forces and a purpose that went beyond mere power.

Late one night, as she pored over the ancient texts, Eva uncovered the true purpose of the spellbook. It was created to contain and control a primordial darkness, a force that had the potential to destroy everything if unleashed. The revelation was both awe-inspiring and terrifying. She knew that mastering the book's power was not just about gaining strength, but about protecting the world from a catastrophic threat.

Seraphina's struggles with dark magic became increasingly apparent. The influence of the forbidden spells had left a mark on her, and she found herself battling inner demons that she had never faced before. Her once confident demeanor was replaced with uncertainty and fear.

One evening, unable to bear it any longer, Seraphina confided in Eva. "I feel like I'm losing myself, Eva. The dark magic... it's consuming me."

Eva's heart ached for her friend. "We'll find a way to help you, Sera. You're not alone in this."

But deep down, Eva knew that the road to recovery would be long and arduous, and she feared that the damage might already be too great to reverse.

Lysander, sensing the growing tension and uncertainty, decided it was time to reveal more about his past and his connection to Professor Voss. Sitting with Eva under the stars, he began to speak of his early days at the academy and the choices that had led him down a dark path.

"Voss was my mentor," Lysander admitted, his voice tinged with regret. "He introduced me to the spellbook, and I was drawn to its power. I thought I could control it, but I was wrong. Voss had his own agenda, and I was just a pawn in his game."

Eva listened, her mind racing. The pieces of the puzzle were beginning to fit together, but the picture they formed was more troubling than she had imagined.

Cassian's influence within the academy continued to grow, causing chaos and dissent. He spread rumors and manipulated students, turning them against Eva and Lysander. His charm and cunning made him a formidable opponent, and his ultimate goal remained shrouded in mystery.

During a tense meeting in the great hall, Cassian confronted Eva. "You think you can lead us, Eva? You're just a girl playing with powers you don't understand."

Eva's eyes blazed with determination. "I'm not afraid of you, Cassian. Your lies won't divide us."

But even as she spoke, she could feel the cracks in the unity she had worked so hard to build.

The strain of their situation began to take a toll on Eva and Lysander's relationship. The constant pressure and external threats tested their bond, and they found themselves arguing more frequently.

One night, after a particularly heated exchange, Lysander took Eva's hand. "I know things are hard right now, but we can't let this tear us apart. We're stronger together."

Eva nodded, her eyes filled with unshed tears. "I know, Lysander. But sometimes it feels like everything is working against us."

Despite their challenges, they both knew that their love was a beacon of hope in the darkness that surrounded them.

Isolde's schemes grew more dangerous as she targeted Eva and Lysander's bond. She spread insidious rumors and manipulated events to sow discord between them. Her jealousy and desire for power drove her to increasingly desperate measures.

During a clandestine meeting, Isolde confronted Lysander. "She'll never understand you like I do, Lysander. You belong with me."

Lysander's eyes were cold. "I chose Eva. Your manipulations won't change that."

Isolde's face twisted with rage. "Then you'll both suffer the consequences."

The threat hung in the air, a dark promise of the challenges yet to come.

Thalia Moonstone, the ancient enchantress, provided crucial information about the spellbook and its creator. She revealed that the book was not just a tool, but a living entity with its own will and purpose.

"The spellbook was created by an ancient sorcerer to contain a great evil," Thalia explained. "But it also has the power to corrupt those who seek to wield it. You must be careful, Eva. The book's power is a double-edged sword."

Eva listened intently, the weight of Thalia's words pressing heavily on her. She realized that the challenges ahead would require not just strength, but wisdom and caution.

The full extent of Gideon Blackwood's role in the dark events of the past came to light. Eva's father had been deeply involved in the creation of the spellbook and the dark magic that it contained. His actions had set in motion the events that now threatened to consume them all.

Eva confronted her father, her voice filled with a mixture of anger and sorrow. "Why didn't you tell me, Father? Why did you keep this from me?"

Gideon's eyes were filled with regret. "I wanted to protect you, Eva. I thought I could keep you safe from the darkness. But I see now that I was wrong."

The revelation left Eva reeling, but it also gave her a new sense of purpose. She was determined to right the wrongs of the past and forge a new path forward.

Eva faced a pivotal moment where she had to decide her true path. The weight of the prophecy, the revelations about her family, and the growing threats all pressed down on her. She stood at a crossroads, knowing that her choice would determine the fate of the academy and everyone she cared about.

Gathering her strength, Eva made her decision. She would embrace her destiny, but on her own terms. She would use the spellbook's power to protect, not to conquer. And she would do it with Lysander and her friends by her side.

As she stepped forward to address the assembled students and faculty, her voice was clear and strong. "We face great challenges, but we will overcome them together. I promise to lead with courage and wisdom, and to protect our academy from the darkness."

The chapter ended with a sense of resolve and determination, as Eva and her allies prepared for the battles yet to come.

Chapter 6: The Temptation

Eva's struggle with her desires reached a critical point. The power within the spellbook called to her, its seductive whispers promising ultimate strength and control. She could feel the darkness growing inside her, a relentless force that threatened to consume her very soul. The temptation was almost too great to resist.

In the solitude of her room, Eva battled her inner demons. She stared at the spellbook, its pages filled with forbidden knowledge, and felt the pull of its power. "I can control it," she whispered to herself. "I have to."

But deep down, she knew the danger. The line between control and corruption was thin, and crossing it could mean losing herself forever.

Lysander sensed Eva's inner turmoil and knew he had to act. He found her in her room, her eyes glazed with the intensity of her internal struggle. "Eva, you have to stop this," he urged, his voice filled with concern. "The power you're playing with is too dangerous."

Eva looked at him, her eyes filled with desperation. "I need it, Lysander. To protect us, to fight the darkness."

Lysander stepped closer, taking her hands in his. "Not like this. We can find another way. You have to trust me."

Eva felt the warmth of his touch, the steadiness of his presence. Slowly, the fog of temptation began to lift, and she saw the danger more clearly. "I trust you," she whispered, leaning into him. "But it's so hard."

Lysander held her tightly, knowing that saving Eva might cost him everything, but willing to risk it all for the woman he loved.

As Eva and Lysander struggled with their own battles, a new dark power began to emerge, threatening the balance of the magical world. Whispers of an ancient force, long thought dormant, began to circulate among the students and faculty. The air seemed to thrum with a sinister energy, and unease spread through the academy like wildfire.

One evening, during a meeting with the academy's leaders, Thalia Moonstone spoke of the growing threat. "We are facing a power unlike any we have encountered before. Its origins are ancient, and its intent is nothing less than total destruction."

The room fell silent, the weight of Thalia's words sinking in. The stakes had never been higher, and the need for unity and strength was more urgent than ever.

Eva and Lysander's love was put to the test as they faced betrayal and sacrifice. The pressures of their situation brought out the best and the worst in them, and they found themselves questioning everything they had built together.

One night, as they prepared for the coming battle, Lysander revealed a painful truth. "Eva, there's something you need to know. I once made a pact with the dark forces. It was a mistake, one I deeply regret, but it may come back to haunt us."

Eva felt a surge of anger and betrayal. "Why didn't you tell me sooner?"

"I was afraid," Lysander admitted. "Afraid of losing you, afraid of what it would mean."

Eva's heart ached with the weight of his confession, but she also understood the depth of his fear. "We have to face this together, Lysander. No more secrets."

Their bond, though tested, remained unbroken. They knew that only by standing united could they hope to overcome the challenges ahead.

Seraphina's role in the unfolding events became more significant. Her struggle with dark magic had given her a unique perspective, and she began to understand how to use her knowledge to help Eva and the academy.

During a strategy meeting, Seraphina spoke up, her voice confident and clear. "I know the darkness better than anyone. Let me help you fight it."

Eva looked at her friend, seeing the determination in her eyes. "We need you, Sera. Together, we can do this."

Seraphina's contribution proved invaluable, her insights and strategies providing a crucial edge in their preparations.

Cassian's ultimate plan was revealed, forcing a showdown. He had been working behind the scenes, gathering power and followers, preparing for a final strike that would cement his control over the academy and its dark magic.

"We will overthrow the current order," Cassian declared to his followers. "With the spellbook's power, we will reshape the magical world."

The time for subtlety was over. Eva and Lysander knew that they had to confront Cassian head-on, and they prepared for a decisive battle that would determine the fate of the academy.

Thalia's guidance proved crucial as Eva struggled with her powers. The ancient enchantress provided insights that helped Eva see a possible way to use her abilities for good, rather than being consumed by them.

"You have a unique gift, Eva," Thalia said, her voice gentle yet firm. "But it is up to you to choose how you use it. The power of the spellbook can be a force for good if wielded with wisdom and restraint."

Eva felt a spark of hope. "Thank you, Thalia. I know what I need to do now."

With Thalia's guidance, Eva began to formulate a plan that could turn the tide in their favor.

The tension between Eva and Isolde reached a boiling point, leading to a dramatic and dangerous confrontation. Isolde, driven by jealousy and a desire for power, targeted Eva and Lysander's bond, hoping to break them apart.

"You think you can defeat me, Eva?" Isolde sneered. "You're nothing without Lysander."

Eva's eyes blazed with determination. "I am stronger than you think, Isolde. And I won't let you tear us apart."

The confrontation was fierce, with spells and enchantments clashing in a dazzling display of power. In the end, Eva's resolve and inner strength prevailed, but the battle left her shaken and more determined than ever to protect those she loved.

The academy's future hung in the balance as Eva's choice loomed large. The preparations for the final confrontation were nearly complete, but the outcome was far from certain. Eva knew that her decisions in the coming days would determine the fate of the academy and the magical world.

In a quiet moment of reflection, Eva stood in the great hall, gazing at the portraits of past leaders. "I will not fail you," she whispered, feeling the weight of history on her shoulders.

Her friends and allies stood by her, ready to face whatever came next. Together, they would fight for their future, no matter the cost.

The chapter ended with Eva making a fateful decision about her powers. She stood before the assembled students and faculty, her voice strong and resolute.

"I have seen the darkness, and I have faced its temptations," she declared. "But I choose to use my power for good, to protect and to heal. Together, we will overcome this threat and rebuild our academy stronger than ever."

Her words were met with a wave of support, the unity of the academy shining through. As the shadows continued to rise, Eva's resolve remained unshaken, her path clear. The battle was far from over, but she knew that with her friends by her side, they could face whatever came next.

Chapter 7: The Forbidden Desire

Eva's decision to embrace her power for good led to immediate and dramatic consequences. The academy buzzed with a renewed sense of purpose, but the dark forces were not willing to concede easily. As Eva and her allies fortified their defenses, the darkness struck back with a vengeance, testing their resolve.

The very air seemed charged with electricity as Eva faced off against the encroaching shadows. Her choice had set off a chain reaction, and the balance of power was shifting rapidly. The students and faculty looked to her for guidance, and she knew that every action she took would have far-reaching implications.

The strain of the battle and the weight of leadership put immense pressure on Eva and Lysander's relationship. They argued more frequently, the stress of their situation bringing their fears and insecurities to the surface.

One night, after a particularly intense confrontation with the dark forces, Lysander confronted Eva. "You're pushing yourself too hard, Eva. We can't afford to lose you."

Eva's eyes flashed with determination. "I have to do this, Lysander. If I don't, everything we've fought for will be for nothing."

The tension between them was palpable, but beneath it lay a deep love and mutual respect. They knew they had to find a way to support each other, or risk being torn apart by the very forces they sought to defeat.

As the battle raged on, the dark power within the spellbook began to threaten Eva's very soul. She could feel its seductive pull, whispering promises of unlimited power and control. The temptation to give in was overwhelming, and she struggled to maintain her grip on reality.

During a moment of weakness, Eva nearly succumbed to the darkness. She felt its cold embrace enveloping her, threatening to consume her entirely. But a vision of her friends and the academy she loved pulled her back from the brink. She knew she had to resist, no matter the cost.

In a dramatic confrontation, Cassian's true nature and motivations were fully revealed. He had always been a master manipulator, but his ultimate goal was far more sinister than anyone had imagined. Cassian sought not just power, but dominion over the entire magical world.

"You're nothing but a pawn, Eva," Cassian sneered. "You think you can control the darkness? It's you who will be controlled."

Eva's anger flared. "I won't let you destroy everything we've fought for."

Cassian's eyes glittered with malice. "We'll see about that."

The revelation of his true nature galvanized Eva and her allies, but it also underscored the gravity of the threat they faced.

Eva's internal battle between desire and duty intensified. The allure of the dark power was a constant presence, and she found herself questioning her every decision. Was she truly strong enough to resist, or would she ultimately fall to its seductive promises?

Thalia's words echoed in her mind: "The power of the spellbook can be a force for good if wielded with wisdom and restraint."

Eva knew that her greatest challenge lay not in the external battles, but within herself. She had to find a way to balance her desires with her duty, or risk losing everything.

Just when things seemed most dire, a surprising ally emerged to help Eva and Lysander. Isolde, who had been an antagonist, had a change of heart. Witnessing the true extent of Cassian's evil, she decided to switch sides and offer her assistance.

"I can't stand by and watch Cassian destroy us all," Isolde admitted. "I want to help."

Lysander was wary, but Eva saw the sincerity in Isolde's eyes. "We need all the help we can get. Thank you, Isolde."

Her unexpected support provided a much-needed boost to their efforts, and her knowledge of dark magic proved invaluable.

Thalia's true identity and her connection to the spellbook were finally uncovered. She was not just an ancient enchantress, but one of the original creators of the spellbook, bound to it by a powerful enchantment.

"I was part of the council that created the spellbook to contain the darkness," Thalia revealed. "But the magic was too strong, and it corrupted many of us."

Her revelation added a new layer of complexity to their struggle. Thalia's insight and experience became crucial as they prepared for the final confrontation.

Gideon Blackwood's redemption arc came to a poignant conclusion. Having been deeply involved in the dark events of the past, he sought to make amends for his actions. In a moment of bravery, he sacrificed himself to protect Eva and the academy from a devastating attack.

"Take care of her," Gideon whispered to Lysander as he lay dying. "She's stronger than she knows."

Eva knelt by her father's side, tears streaming down her face. "I forgive you, Father. Thank you."

His death was a heavy blow, but it also gave Eva a renewed sense of purpose. She was determined to honor his sacrifice and ensure that his mistakes were not repeated.

The final battle between light and dark forces began. The academy grounds were transformed into a war zone, with spells and enchantments lighting up the night sky. Eva and Lysander fought side by side, their love and unity giving them strength.

Cassian, now fully revealed as the embodiment of the dark power, unleashed his fury upon them. "You cannot defeat me," he roared. "The darkness is eternal."

Eva felt the weight of the prophecy and the power within her. She knew that this was the moment she had been preparing for, the culmination of all her struggles and sacrifices.

The chapter ended with a cliffhanger as Eva's ultimate fate remained uncertain. In a desperate move, she began to channel the full power of the spellbook, risking everything to defeat Cassian once and for all. The ground shook, and the air crackled with magical energy.

As the light and dark forces clashed, Eva's friends watched in awe and fear. The outcome of the battle, and Eva's fate, hung in the balance. The future of the academy and the magical world was on the line, and the next moments would determine everything.

Chapter 8: The Redemption

The battle reached its peak, with the fate of the academy and the magical world hanging in the balance. The air was thick with the clash of spells and the cries of the wounded. Eva stood at the center of the chaos, her heart pounding as she channeled the full power of the spellbook.

Cassian, his eyes blazing with malevolent energy, loomed before her. "You cannot win, Eva. The darkness is eternal."

Eva felt the weight of his words, but she refused to back down. "We'll see about that," she replied, her voice filled with determination.

As the ground trembled and the sky darkened, the stakes were higher than ever. Every decision, every spell, could mean the difference between victory and defeat.

Eva and Lysander fought side by side, their bond a beacon of hope in the midst of the battle. Their movements were perfectly synchronized, each one anticipating the other's needs and actions. They were a formidable team, their love and unity giving them strength.

In the heat of the battle, they found moments of closeness that fueled their resolve. Between casting spells and dodging attacks, they would exchange quick, passionate kisses, a reminder of what they were fighting for.

"Stay with me," Lysander whispered, his eyes locking with Eva's during a brief respite.

"Always," she replied, her heart swelling with love and determination.

Their love was a light in the darkness, a force that drove them to keep fighting, no matter the odds.

Seraphina's role in the battle proved crucial. Drawing on her deep knowledge of dark magic, she devised strategies that helped turn the tide. Her spells were precise and powerful, targeting the weaknesses of the dark forces.

At a critical moment, Seraphina unleashed a spell that disrupted Cassian's control over his followers, creating a window of opportunity for Eva and Lysander to press their advantage.

"Now, Eva!" Seraphina shouted, her voice cutting through the chaos.

Eva seized the moment, channeling her power into a devastating attack that sent Cassian reeling. Seraphina's contribution was vital, and it showed how far she had come from her struggles with dark magic.

Cassian's downfall was inevitable. As his control slipped, he became increasingly desperate, lashing out with reckless fury. His once charismatic and manipulative demeanor gave way to raw, uncontained rage.

"You've lost, Cassian," Eva declared, her voice steady and resolute. "Your reign of terror ends here."

Cassian's eyes widened with fear and realization. "No, this can't be happening!"

With one final, powerful spell, Eva and Lysander combined their energies to defeat Cassian, his form dissolving into nothingness. The consequences of his actions rippled through the battlefield, his followers disoriented and leaderless.

Isolde made a final, desperate attempt to reclaim Lysander. Driven by jealousy and a twisted sense of love, she confronted Eva, determined to eliminate her rival.

"Lysander belongs to me," Isolde hissed, her eyes blazing with fury. "I won't let you take him from me!"

Eva stood her ground, her resolve unshaken. "Lysander made his choice, Isolde. It's over."

Their confrontation was intense, spells clashing in a dazzling display of power. In the end, Eva's strength and determination prevailed. Isolde fell, her ambitions shattered, and Lysander rushed to Eva's side.

"You did it," he murmured, pulling her into a tight embrace.

"We did it," Eva corrected, her heart full.

Thalia's true purpose was revealed in a moment of great sacrifice. She had been guiding Eva and her friends not just as an enchantress, but as a guardian bound to the spellbook's fate. Her final act was to use her life force to seal the dark power within the book, ensuring it could never be unleashed again.

"Thank you, Thalia," Eva whispered, tears streaming down her face as Thalia's form began to fade.

"Remember, Eva," Thalia said softly. "The true power lies within you."

With Thalia's sacrifice, the dark magic was contained, but the cost was great. Her loss was deeply felt, but her legacy lived on through Eva and her friends.

Eva's final confrontation with the dark power within her was the ultimate test. She stood alone, facing the embodiment of the darkness that had plagued her. It was a battle of wills, a struggle to maintain her identity and purpose.

"You cannot control me," the dark power taunted. "You are weak, just like the others."

Eva took a deep breath, centering herself. "I am not weak. I am stronger than you can imagine."

Drawing on the love and support of her friends, and the lessons she had learned, Eva channeled her inner light. The darkness resisted, but she remained steadfast, ultimately vanquishing the dark power and reclaiming her true self.

Lysander's ultimate act of love and sacrifice was to save Eva. As the battle reached its climax, he placed himself in harm's way to protect her, taking a deadly blow meant for her. His love for Eva gave him the strength to endure, but the cost was high.

"Stay with me, Lysander," Eva pleaded, tears streaming down her face. "I can't lose you."

Lysander's hand brushed her cheek, his touch gentle despite his pain. "I'll always be with you, Eva. No matter what."

His sacrifice was a testament to their love, a beacon of hope even in the darkest moments. Eva's heart ached with the depth of her loss, but she knew that Lysander's spirit would always be with her.

The resolution of the battle and the restoration of balance were hard-won. The dark forces were defeated, and the academy began the long process of healing and rebuilding. The students and faculty, though scarred by the conflict, found new strength in their unity and resilience.

Eva stood before the assembled students and faculty, her voice clear and strong. "We have faced great challenges and endured tremendous loss, but we have also found strength and hope. Together, we will rebuild and ensure that the darkness never threatens us again."

The sense of hope and renewal was palpable, a testament to the power of love, unity, and determination.

The chapter ended with Eva and Lysander finding peace and hope for the future. In a quiet moment, they stood together in the academy's gardens, the beauty of the flowers and the tranquility of the setting a stark contrast to the chaos they had faced.

Eva turned to Lysander, her heart full. "We did it. We survived."

Lysander smiled, pulling her close. "We did. And now we can look forward to a future filled with hope and love."

Their bond, tested and strengthened by their trials, was a beacon of light for the future. As they embraced, they knew that whatever challenges lay ahead, they would face them together, their love a guiding force in the darkness.

Chapter 9: A New Dawn

The aftermath of the battle left the academy in a state of both physical and emotional upheaval. The grounds were scarred, and the echoes of conflict lingered in the hearts of the students and faculty. Yet, amid the rubble and the wreckage, there was a profound sense of unity and hope.

Eva, now a recognized leader, spearheaded the efforts to rebuild. She worked tirelessly alongside her friends, each act of restoration a testament to their resilience and determination. The magical academy, once a battleground, began to transform into a symbol of renewal and strength.

As the days turned into weeks, Eva found herself reflecting on her journey. She had grown immensely, both as a witch and as a person. The trials she had faced had forged her into a leader, and she felt a deep sense of pride and gratitude for the experiences that had shaped her.

One evening, as the sun set over the academy, Eva stood on the balcony of her room, gazing out at the horizon. The sky was a canvas of vibrant colors, a reminder of the beauty and promise of each new day.

Lysander joined her, wrapping his arms around her from behind. "What are you thinking about?" he asked softly.

Eva leaned back into his embrace, a smile playing on her lips. "Everything we've been through. How far we've come."

Lysander pressed a kiss to her temple. "You've grown so much, Eva. I'm proud of you."

Eva turned in his arms, their faces inches apart. "And I couldn't have done it without you."

Their lips met in a passionate kiss, a celebration of their journey and their love. The intimacy they shared was a powerful reminder of the bond that had sustained them through the darkest times.

Lysander's redemption was a journey of its own. He had faced his past and emerged stronger, ready to take on a new role in the magical world. As a mentor and protector, he dedicated himself to guiding the next generation of witches and wizards, ensuring that the mistakes of the past would not be repeated.

During a ceremony to honor the heroes of the battle, Lysander was recognized for his bravery and leadership. The students and faculty applauded him, their respect and admiration evident.

Eva stood beside him, her heart swelling with pride. "You deserve this, Lysander. You've come so far."

Lysander squeezed her hand, his eyes shining with gratitude. "And I owe it all to you, Eva."

Their love, tested and strengthened by their trials, was a beacon of hope for the future.

Seraphina found a new path, her experiences with dark magic giving her a unique perspective and purpose. She decided to dedicate herself to studying and teaching about the dangers and complexities of forbidden spells, ensuring that others would learn from her journey.

Eva and Seraphina's friendship remained strong, their bond unbreakable despite the challenges they had faced. They often spent evenings together, reminiscing about their adventures and planning for the future.

One night, as they sat by the fire, Seraphina turned to Eva. "I'm grateful for you, Eva. You've always been there for me."

Eva smiled, reaching out to clasp Seraphina's hand. "And I always will be. We're in this together, Sera."

Their friendship was a testament to the power of loyalty and support, a reminder that even in the darkest times, they had each other.

Thalia's legacy was one of wisdom and sacrifice. Her guidance had been crucial in their victory, and her teachings continued to inspire the students of the academy. A memorial was erected in her honor, a tribute to her dedication and the impact she had made.

Eva often visited the memorial, finding solace in the memories of Thalia's guidance. One day, as she stood before the statue, she felt a sense of peace and purpose.

"Thank you, Thalia," she whispered. "For everything."

Thalia's legacy lived on through Eva and her friends, a guiding light that would continue to shine for generations to come.

Gideon Blackwood's reconciliation with Eva was a poignant moment of healing and forgiveness. He had played a complex role in the events that had unfolded, and his journey towards redemption was marked by his desire to make amends.

Eva and Gideon spent time together, rebuilding their relationship and finding common ground. Through their conversations, they found a deeper understanding of each other and the choices they had made.

One afternoon, as they walked through the academy gardens, Gideon turned to Eva. "I'm proud of you, Eva. You've become a remarkable leader."

Eva smiled, her heart full. "Thank you, Father. I'm glad we could find our way back to each other."

Gideon's new purpose was to support Eva and contribute to the academy's future, his redemption a testament to the power of forgiveness and change.

The magical academy underwent a transformation, emerging from the shadows of its past into a beacon of hope and knowledge. New leadership, inspired by the trials they had faced, guided the institution with wisdom and vision.

Eva was appointed as the head of the academy, her leadership a reflection of her strength and dedication. Under her guidance, the academy flourished, becoming a place where young witches and wizards could learn and grow in a safe and supportive environment.

The students, once fearful and uncertain, now thrived under Eva's leadership. The academy was not just a place of learning, but a community united by their shared experiences and goals.

Eva and Lysander's future together was filled with hope and possibility. They had faced unimaginable challenges and emerged stronger, their love a testament to their resilience and commitment.

In the privacy of their home, they found moments of intimacy and connection that were a source of joy and comfort. Their nights were filled with passionate embraces and whispered promises, their love a constant source of strength.

One evening, as they lay together, Lysander brushed a strand of hair from Eva's face. "We've been through so much, but I wouldn't trade it for anything."

Eva smiled, her heart full. "Neither would I. Our future is bright, Lysander. I can't wait to see what comes next."

Their bond, unbreakable and eternal, was a beacon of hope for the future.

The final resolution of lingering conflicts brought a sense of peace and closure. The academy, once divided by fear and uncertainty, was now united in purpose and vision. The dark forces that had threatened them were vanquished, and the promise of peace was within reach.

Eva stood before the assembled students and faculty, her voice filled with hope and determination. "We have faced great challenges and endured tremendous loss, but we have also found strength and hope. Together, we will build a brighter future."

The sense of unity and renewal was palpable, a testament to their resilience and determination.

The chapter ended with a hopeful and inspiring note, looking towards a brighter future. Eva and Lysander, standing together, looked out over the academy they had worked so hard to protect.

"We've come so far," Eva said softly, her heart full.

"And we have so much to look forward to," Lysander replied, his arm around her shoulders.

Their love, tested and strengthened by their trials, was a beacon of light for the future. As they embraced, they knew that whatever challenges lay ahead, they would face them together, their love a guiding force in the darkness.

Chapter 10: Epilogue

Years had passed since the great battle, and the magical world had been forever changed by Eva and Lysander's journey. The academy had been rebuilt and transformed into a beacon of hope and knowledge. The scars of the past had healed, and the future was bright with promise.

Eva, now a respected leader in the magical community, often reflected on the journey that had brought her here. Her days were filled with teaching, mentoring, and guiding the next generation of witches and wizards. She found immense satisfaction in seeing her students grow and flourish, knowing that the lessons she imparted would shape the future of the magical world.

Lysander, too, had found his place in this new era. As a prominent figure in the magical council, he worked tirelessly to ensure that the principles of balance and harmony were upheld. Together, they had become a symbol of hope and resilience, their love story inspiring all who knew them.

The legacy of the spellbook was a complex one. It had brought great challenges, but also invaluable lessons. Eva ensured that its history and power were not forgotten but used as a tool for learning and growth. The students were taught about its dangers and its potential, fostering a deep respect for the balance between light and dark.

In the library, a special section was dedicated to the spellbook and its teachings. Eva often visited this place, reflecting on the journey that had brought them here.

One afternoon, she spoke to a group of students. "The spellbook is a reminder that power comes with responsibility. We must use our gifts wisely, always mindful of the consequences."

Her words were met with thoughtful nods, the students understanding the gravity of her message.

The magical world had entered a new era of harmony and understanding. Witches and wizards from diverse backgrounds and traditions came together, united by a common goal of peace and progress. The divisions that once plagued their society were healed and replaced by a spirit of collaboration and mutual respect.

Eva and Lysander played a pivotal role in this transformation, their leadership and vision guiding the magical community towards a brighter future. They traveled to different magical enclaves, spreading their message of unity and balance.

During one such visit, an elder wizard approached them. "Your journey has inspired us all. Thank you for showing us the way."

Eva smiled, her heart swelling with gratitude. "It's a journey we all share. Together, we can achieve anything."

Eva and Lysander's love continued to be a source of strength and inspiration. Their bond, forged in the fires of battle and tested by countless challenges, remained unbreakable. They supported each other in all things, and their love was a guiding light for their future.

In the privacy of their home, they found moments of deep intimacy and connection. Their nights were filled with passionate embraces and whispered promises, their love a constant source of joy and comfort.

One evening, after a long day of work, Lysander pulled Eva into his arms. "You are my everything," he whispered, his lips brushing against her ear.

Eva shivered with delight, her heart racing. "And you are mine," she replied, their bodies entwined in a dance of love and desire.

Their lovemaking was a symphony of passion and tenderness, each touch and kiss a reaffirmation of their unbreakable bond. As they lay entwined, their bodies glistening with the sheen of their exertions, they whispered sweet nothings to each other, their love a beacon of hope in the darkness.

Seraphina's adventures continued, her curiosity and bravery leading her to discoveries. She became a renowned scholar, her work on dark magic and its complexities earning her respect and admiration. Her friendship with Eva remained strong, their bond a testament to their shared experiences and mutual support.

During a visit to the academy, Seraphina shared her latest findings with Eva. "I've discovered a new way to neutralize dark magic without harming the caster," she said excitedly.

Eva's eyes sparkled with pride. "That's incredible, Sera. Your work is changing the world."

Seraphina smiled; her heart full. "And it's all thanks to you. You believed in me when no one else did."

Their friendship was a beacon of hope and inspiration, a reminder that together, they could achieve anything.

The memories of Thalia continued to inspire and guide them. Her teachings and sacrifices were honored and remembered, her legacy a cornerstone of the academy's philosophy. Thalia's wisdom was a constant presence, her lessons woven into the fabric of their lives.

Eva often visited the memorial garden dedicated to Thalia, finding solace and inspiration in the peaceful surroundings. One day, she brought a group of students to the garden, sharing stories of Thalia's bravery and wisdom.

"Thalia taught us that true strength comes from within," Eva said, her voice filled with reverence. "Her legacy lives on in each of us."

The students listened intently; their hearts touched by Thalia's enduring influence.

The reconciliation of past conflicts and the unity of the magical community were celebrated with a grand festival. Witches and wizards from all over the world gathered to honor the journey they had shared and the peace they had achieved.

Eva and Lysander stood at the forefront of the celebration, their hearts swelling with pride and joy. They watched as old enemies embraced, new friendships were formed, and the spirit of unity filled the air.

Gideon Blackwood, now fully reconciled with his daughter, stood by their side. "This is what we've worked for," he said, his voice choked with emotion. "A future where we are all united."

Eva nodded, tears of happiness in her eyes. "It's a new dawn for us all."

Eva's last thoughts were filled with hope and vision for a world balanced between light and dark. She understood that the journey was ongoing and that they must remain vigilant and committed to their ideals.

Standing before the assembled magical community, Eva shared her vision. "We have come a long way, but our journey is not over. We must continue to strive for balance, to honor the lessons of the past, and to build a future where light and dark coexist in harmony."

Her words were met with resounding applause, the community united in their commitment to a brighter future.

A final, tender moment between Eva and Lysander symbolized their journey and the love that had sustained them. They stood together in their garden, the moon casting a soft glow over their surroundings.

Lysander took Eva's hands in his, his eyes filled with love and devotion. "We did it, Eva. We've built something beautiful."

Eva leaned in, her lips brushing against his. "And we'll continue to build, together."

Their kiss was a promise of all that was to come, their love a beacon of hope and possibility. They moved to the privacy of their bedroom, where their passion ignited once more. Their lovemaking was a dance of love and desire, each touch and caress a testament to their unbreakable bond.

Lysander gently pushed Eva onto the bed, his hands exploring her body with a mix of tenderness and urgency. "You are so beautiful," he whispered, his lips trailing down her neck.

Eva moaned softly, her body responding to his touch. "I need you, Lysander," she breathed, pulling him closer.

Their clothes fell away, and they were soon lost in a world of sensation. Lysander's touch was both gentle and possessive, his hands and mouth worshipping Eva's body. Eva arched beneath him, their connection deepening with each caress and kiss.

"You're mine," Lysander whispered, his voice thick with desire.

"Always," Eva replied, their bodies moving together in a perfect rhythm.

Their lovemaking was intense and passionate, a testament to the love and trust they shared. As they reached their climax, their cries of pleasure filled the room, a beautiful symphony of their unity.

Afterward, they lay entwined, their bodies glistening with the sheen of their exertions. Lysander brushed a strand of hair from Eva's face, his eyes filled with love. "I love you, Eva."

Eva smiled; her heart full. "And I love you, Lysander. Forever."

About the Author

Hi! I'm Sheila Mae Ilano, a fantasy romance writer from the Philippines. Inspired by the magical worlds created by J.K. Rowling, I love weaving tales of enchantment, love, and adventure. When I'm not lost in writing, you'll find me with my nose buried in a book, exploring new realms and characters. Join me on a journey through the mystical and romantic landscapes of my imagination. Happy reading! ◈ ◈